This book
belongs to

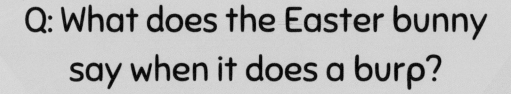

Q: What does the Easter bunny say when it does a burp?

Q: Why don't you see dinosaurs at Easter?

A: Because they are eggs-tinct!

Q: How does the Easter bunny stay in shape?

Q: What did the egg say when the Easter bunny told a joke?

Q: What do you call the Easter bunny the day after Easter?

A: Eggshausted.

Q: What do you call an Easter egg from outer space?

Q: What did the chocolate bunny say when its ear had been bitten?

Q: Why did the Easter egg hide?

Q: Why was the Easter bunny so upset?

A: He was having a bad hare day!

Q: What did the bunny want to do when he grew up?

A: Join the hare force!

Q: What do you call a bunny that tells jokes?

A: A funny bunny!

Q: What do you call a bunny with a big brain?

Q: How did the bunny get out of the building?

Q: What do you call a rabbit with sniffles?

Q: What do you say to the bunny on its birthday?

A: Hoppy birthday!

Q: Where do bunnies go when they are sick?

A: To the hopspital!

Q: How did the Easter bunny rate the Easter parade?

A: Eggs-cellent!

Q: What day does an Easter egg hate the most?

Q: What did the egg do in the car when the light turned green?

Q: Did you hear the one about the house infested with Easter eggs?

A: It needed an eggs-terminator!

Q: How does the Easter bunny feel on the night before Easter?

Q: Why did the Easter bunny cross the road?

Q: How does a bunny keep his hair looking good?

A: With hare spray!

Q: What happened when the Easter Bunny fell in love with another bunny?

A: They lived hoppily ever after.

Q: Why did the Easter bunny go to school?

A: To get egg-ducated.

Q: What do bunnies do after a wedding?

Q: What did the bunny ask his friend?

Q: What books did the easter bunny like the most?

A: Ones with a hoppy ending!

happy easter!

I read and appreciate all of my reviews. I would be grateful if you could take a minute to leave one!

Simply visit
amazon.co.uk/review/create-review?&asin=B08VR7QKNN

Or scan ⟶

Simply open up your camera on your smart phone and scan to take you to the page!

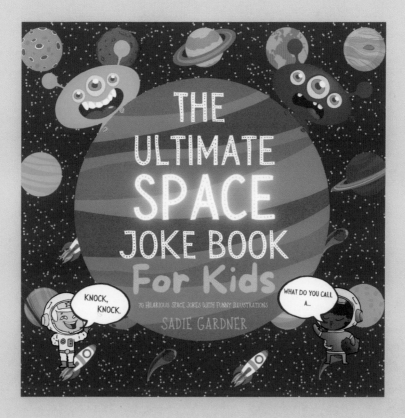

The Ultimate Space Joke Book For Kids!
Heaps of hilarious space jokes coupled with funny illustrations, providing hours of entertainment for kids of any age – even adults!
This must-get joke book includes:
Hilarious space, alien and astronaut jokes.
Knock-knock Jokes.
Humorous illustrations.
A fun challenge at the back to do with your friends and family!
This makes a perfect gift for kids as the funny characters and jokes will guarantee to put a smile on their face.
Grab your copy today and have an 'out of this world' giggle!

amazon.co.uk/Ultimate-Space-Joke-Book-Kids-ebook/dp/B08YKC0S27

Or scan

Check out my other books

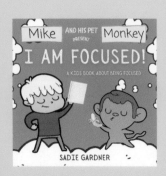

Visit

amazon.com/Sadie-Gardner/e/B086VMTLNM

Or scan $\longrightarrow$

Printed in Great Britain
by Amazon

20356738R00025